MIDNIGHT HEATWAVE

A SILVER RAPIDS NOVELLA

ANASTASIA WILDER

Midnight Shadows Press

Contents

DEDICATION

For the ones who were too much and never enough, do what the fuck makes your heart sing.

TUNES & ART

MAVERICK
BENNETT
CHARLOTTE
ADLER

CHAPTER 1

CHARLOTTE

"**C**harlie, you better get that fine little ass down here. Let's go!" My friend Quinn calls from the first floor of my house.

"Hold your horses, I'm almost ready," I shout down to her. I glance back to my reflection in the mirror and take in my long blonde curls that are finally sitting right. I never curl my hair anymore. There's no reason to when you work on a cattle ranch.

Technically, my house is a rental. Mother would absolutely die if she knew that I was renting. "Just throwing away money when you could own. Buy real estate and make others pay YOU rent." It's the Adler way. My family are real estate moguls back east. But the last thing I want is my name permanently tied to anything.

When I moved in, the only request I really had out of any landlord was that they were pet-friendly, so I could adopt a dog at some point. I haven't found the right one, but I'll know when I see her or him, I suppose.

I hear Quinn bouncing up the stairs, the slight twang of her southern drawl coming out after the few pre-gaming cocktails we had while we were getting ready for a night out. I'm not about to pay bar prices when I have plenty of booze here. "Charlie! You look incredible in that getup. Look at that fringe!"

She's not wrong. The smoky blue-green fringe pants and matching cropped bralette that I'm wearing have hundreds of little strands flowing and swishing about every time I move so much as an inch. I used to wear things like this back in Boston whenever I'd go out with friends. Back then it wasn't fancy, it was expected. Cocktails on a rooftop, dinner in Little Italy, or brunch in Somerville. Now, it's like armor. Like dressing up in something you know looks good gives you the confidence you might have lost along the way. And it brings out the blue in my eyes.

Quinn is wearing a short, ripped-hem, dark blue denim skirt. On top she's got a cute, white lace bralette and an unbuttoned pink and white gingham flannel that's tied at her waist. I learned a lot about cowboy boots when I moved here. She's in white embroidered Ariats that come up to her mid-calf. She looks like a Western pin-up girl with her dark brown, curled hair that's pinned back and pink lips.

"I just need a pair of shoes and a bag, then we can head out."

"The men of Silver Rapids aren't going to know what swept into town when they see you in this," Quinn exclaims.

"Ha! I'm not looking for a man tonight." Truthfully, I just wanted to put on an outfit that made me feel good. I mutter to myself, "That's the last thing I need. No men." Quinn just smirks and shakes her head. I'm looking right at her when I say, "Seriously! Now help me pick out a pair of shoes."

We head into my bedroom and to my closet. She picks up a few different pairs of stilettos and then moves on to booties and my cowboy boots. She picks up a pair of rhinestone booties with a chunky heel. "Are these comfortable? Like you can dance and run in them?"

"Run?!" I shriek. "What the hell kind of trouble do you have planned for tonight? I thought this was like a summer kickoff kind of weekend. I will not be running because there is no drama tonight." Crossing my arms, I look at my friend warily.

Quinn is the first person I've really connected with since moving to Wyoming. We met a little over five months ago. On my third day in town, she saw me circling the racks at the small bookstore where she works and asked what kind of story I wanted. She ended up selling me three romance novels and a self-help book. We've been friends ever since. It's been nice having someone to meet up with for dinner or brunch dates after long days at the ranch. She's from the Dallas area and we're the outliers in town. Everyone else is from here and, like the tornado from Oz, she and I just ended up here.

"You never know where the night will lead us, babes." She winks and tosses the silver rhinestone booties towards the bed. They land with a thunk, and she points and says, "Put those on. They're so cute!" I grin at her and walk over to the bed to put them on. She pulls a clear acrylic wristlet with a gold zipper and chain to go around my wrist. "Fuck me runnin', we're going full city girl tonight." She whoops and flops on the bed beside me. I'm already tired.

Shoes securely on my feet, we head down to the kitchen for one more rosy-lemon shot. It's limoncello, vodka, muddled rosemary leaves, and soda water. It's a fave from one of my old Little Italy haunts. There was a time when my old friends and I would order dozens of these and stay by the pool at my parents' club all day.

"To a night we'll always remember!" We clink glasses, tap them to the table and take the shot back in one gulp. The mix of the sweet and tart of the drink warms my throat on the way down.

"Cheers to that, baby girl," Quinn replies.

We head out of the house and start walking towards town. My house isn't too far from the downtown area and I'm used to walking every-where. I asked Quinn if we should drive and then walk back, but she said there was something to be said about walking back home and sobering just enough to pop a pizza in the oven before we pass out. What a clever girl. Is there anything better than the perfect buzz, a belly full of pizza, and a comfy bed? Okay, a lot of things are better, but as nights out go. That's pretty fantastic.

Quinn moans and I look over to her. She says, "I could definitely go for some cotton candy. Oh, or some fried Oreos."

"Yes to cotton candy and lemonade. Mmm." I say as I rub my belly.

Quinn asks, "We haven't even talked about your new job, missy! Are you settling in okay? What exactly are you doing with horses?"

I laugh. I explained my new role to her when I accepted it two weeks ago. "I help muck stalls, feed and brush the horses, and ride them a bit for exercise. Or I unload the hay, grain, and bed shavings. Just kind of help the owner. I told him when we talked that I only ever rode English style and that I have never built anything in my life, so I wouldn't be able to help him fix the fences or anything like that."

"Have you ever worked with animals before?"

"Kind of," I reply. If you consider the men in investment banking animals. Which, I do. I can never explain to her what I used to do for work. That in a different life, I managed a top-performing hedge fund back home. That more money passed through my hands than water running out of a faucet. If I wasn't worried about my skeletons finding me, I wouldn't really have to work. But, I only have so much cash left from what I brought with me. I don't want to use any debit or credit cards, nothing that can be traced back to me. It's better for everyone if that part of my life stays buried, locked in a box that will never see the sunlight again. "But I'm excited to learn something new."

"So long as mucking stalls makes you happy, Charlie," she shudders. "Blech."

"I love horses. I've spent my entire life around them." *And the ranch owner said he would pay me in cash.*

"Honey, I think they're gorgeous, beautiful creatures. So long as they're far from me."

I giggle, "You're from Texas. How can you not like horses?"

"I think maybe it's their eyes, they see too much. And they can kill you if they trample or throw you." She's not wrong. I've seen a few accidents, but isn't that part of the allure of horses? Feeling the power of nature harnessed in a grand and noble animal that could literally kill you with one wrong move? I'm a slight adrenaline junkie.

After another ten minutes of chatting, we see the barricades up ahead that block off Main Street. All of the shops are closed for the festival, allowing their employees to join in the festivities with their friends and families.

The quaint town of Silver Rapids is nestled in the heart of Western Wyoming. Brick-faced buildings line the street, each of them unique and full of charm. That's why I stayed here instead of moving on. The charisma and people of the town were so kind and welcoming.

The diner, The Bluebird, on the corner of Main and 5th, has a wall of windows that wrap around the side starting from the front door. A blue neon "Open" sign is on just above it. On the side of the building, there's an old mural of an elk dipping its head to a small river with rapids that's faded with time and age. You can tell that it was impressive once. But I think that to paint over it, even if it were a perfect replica, would take away from the appeal of it. The diner is packed with locals and visitors alike. They have the best homemade cheesecakes and pies.

We walk past the door as someone walks out, and Quinn groans, "Mmmm, everything smells so dang good!"

The town has absolutely come alive. People have come from all across the county and beyond for the festival. Main and North Streets are full of artisans and craft vendors selling baked goods and self-care products. I note that there are some pop-up boutiques selling handcrafted jewelry and vintage, boho clothing that we walk past before we get to the good stuff: the carnival food.

The sun is giving us a great show tonight. The sky is the most brilliant color of blues, pinks, and lavenders with soft clouds high in the sky. Golden light is giving its Midas touch to everything it lands on, bathing the storefronts and carnival stands in warmth. We pass The Book Nook just past the diner, and Quinn waves hello to the books on display in the window. We continue on to see the whole street decked out in festive banners strung from one side of the street to the other.

There is something so majestic about golden hour. The whole world is bathed in an amber glow. Even the snow-capped mountains in the distance are brilliantly shining and reflecting the sun's setting rays. I look down to my feet and they look like disco balls, light reflecting off them in a million different directions.

We are making our way down to North where the food stalls are; a mix of sausages and hot dogs, homemade pies, fried snacks like churros, and deep-fried Oreos. When I round the corner, I see a mechanical bull setup. "Yes! Absolutely, yes! We are doing this," I squeal and clap with excitement.

"No, absolutely not." Quinn freezes on the sidewalk. "Nope. Not happening."

"Oh, we absolutely are," I say. I grab her arm and pull her along with me towards the bullpen.

CHAPTER 2

MAVERICK

The guys and I exit Caleb's mom's bakery, The Flour Child, to the street filled with carnival goers from all over Wyoming. The festival gets bigger every year. Sometimes being back here isn't so bad, to see how much it's changed from when I left. It's been fourteen months since I've last been home. The time between visits is getting longer and longer and, as much as I love Dad, we're too different. I want different things for my life than what he wants for me. The last time I was here, I was preparing for the Olympic trials. I went to Vail, then *that* happened and I didn't need to come back here to feel everyone's eyes on me.

I only came back because Caleb wanted to get the old crew together for a small, hometown bachelor party. His younger brother, Jake, has developmental disabilities, so new places can be hard for him. Jake is a few years younger, but where Caleb went, Jake followed. He was always with us, tagging along, watching us get into stupid shit, and laughing when we'd get caught. In school, I looked after Jake like he was my own little brother. After Mom died, Mrs. Clark kept an eye on me and Dad. Coming home to visit with them, and I guess Dad, was the least I could do when Caleb said that he wanted a small party to celebrate. So the boys rallied and headed home for the long weekend.

Caleb went to Colorado State University on a football scholarship but majored in business so that he could return back to Silver Rapids and help his mom grow her bakery. Garret went to Notre Dame for lacrosse and stayed out in the Midwest after he graduated. He works in accounting, but jokes that it's not the spicy kind. He said he was moving back home soon. I went to CSU for business through their online program. I would go visit Caleb in Fort Collins often though, it was only a few hours from Vail or Aspen. Luke moved to town our junior year of high school. He didn't go to college but started his own construction company and now builds anything with four walls and a roof.

We knew that Caleb was going to be the first of us to pair off. He has had heart eyes for Kennedy since the second day of senior year of high school when he saved her from falling down the stairs in the hallway when somebody rushed past her. It was his real-life superhero moment. I've never had one of those, no surprise there. I've never dated anyone seriously. When I do start to feel the spark of an ember with someone, it falls apart before it really ever begun. Not that the relationships I've had have been meaningless, when I'm with someone I am only with them, they just tend to run hot and fast like a firework, a bright flash in a dark sky. But Caleb? He's in it for life and to be honest, I love that life for him. He deserves it. I'm thinking that I deserve to be a miserable asshole after everything.

"Let's go get some food!" Caleb declares.

"You just had two pieces of pie, my man." Garrett laughs.

"I could eat," I say. "Let's see what we find."

And that's when I see a mass of waist-length, golden curls reflecting the light of the sun like a halo around a beautiful woman walking our way. She's laughing and her smile, it's megawatt blinding. She's wearing something that looks like a bathing suit top, but it's got lots of fringe hanging from it, and it stops just below her breasts. Her toned stomach is a bare expanse of smooth skin. The flare of her hips could be my undoing. The pants are the same type of material as her top. The thousand little strings flit about accenting her long legs and look like waves pulling back and forth on the sand as she walks toward me. In that outfit, she is definitely not from Silver Rapids. What's on her feet? Mirrored boots? They look like they're glowing. This woman is not from here. She might not even be from this planet.

With her is a striking brunette who is laughing at something the blonde woman says. Have they put something in the water supply to make the women here even more ravishing since I left?

She and her friend are headed to the mechanical bull. No. No way. Are they going to try to beat Brutus? Brutus is the bull that's usually in Bart's bar. I've been bucked off that damn thing too many times to count. Old Man Bart thinks it's hilarious and makes it his mission to knock people off. Just when you think you might go the full eight seconds, no. He gives the controls a kick into overdrive and bam! You're in the corner with a bruised ego, holding a beer to your busted lip. I don't want them to get injured, but I do want a front-row seat to that show. "Hey guys, let's do the bull before we eat. The last thing we need is for Caleb to pop on top of Brutus again."

"Bro, not cool. It was one time and to be fair, I don't remember it." Caleb pouts and crosses his arms but we head that way.

I see the girls go to the signup booth. The blonde is clearly excited and the brunette has a scowl across her face. We are walking towards the bull when Garrett laughs and elbows me in the ribs.

"Dude. You haven't changed." Garrett's looking towards Blondie and her friend. "You could have just said hotties at two o'clock. The brunette is Quinn. She moved here a year or so ago. She works at the bookstore, and Luke called dibs. The blonde I've seen a few times during my visits in the last few months, but I don't know anything about her. But if she's single, I call dibs!"

"Call dibs? What are we, ten years old? Dibs doesn't count."

"Well, we'll see who she's more interested in, eh?"

There's a group of people walking our way that move over to the road. Our group takes up a lot of space on the sidewalk. Luke is the shortest, but just by inches. He was a runt and then one summer filled out just like the rest of us. He's also the one with tattoos, full arm sleeves, chest and back pieces, the guy is covered. Some people in town think it's intimidating, but I think it's art. Garrett, having played lacrosse for so long, is stacked. Jake, for all of his quirks, regularly goes to the gym with Caleb and Luke.

Being here has me feeling a little left out of the antics Caleb and Luke get into. My best friend back in Utah, Jude, hits the gym with me every day. He's a cattle rancher but he does a lot of horseback tours from spring to fall. We have plans this year to try our hand at skijoring. He'll be atop his horse, barreling down a snow-covered street, pulling me through a course with a tow rope as I ski over jumps and through slalom gates. The sport has been around since the early 1900s in Northern Europe with roots in harnessing reindeer to take people over distances, kind of like sled dog racing in Alaska. But with horses, fire, and ring jousting. If you do the circuit right, there's a lot of money in competing.

Since losing all my sponsorships, it's been kind of tight. Working full-time as a ski instructor doesn't pay as well as you think. I get a salary, but make a lot off of tips as well. I suppose I could do something with my business degree, but I've never had a real job before. It's not even Peter Pan syndrome, I've just never had an opportunity to have a job. I spent all my time up on the mountain or in the gym training. Before that, I was helping Dad.

Quinn and her friend are still talking to the ticket booth attendant when me and the guys walk up behind them. I can hear the guys excitedly talking about who is going to go the full eight seconds this time.

"I'm definitely gonna go the full eight seconds," says Luke.

Laughing, Garrett says, "Ha! I'll believe that when I see it."

"You both are delusional. I'm going to be the one to go for the full eight seconds," I toss back over my shoulder.

The blonde and her friend turn back to us, size us up, and say, "Alright boys, but we're up first."

"Not 'we', just you, babycakes!" laughs Quinn to her friend.

Blondie just scowls and blows a raspberry at her friend and walks over to the roped off entrance. I am just a man, so when she starts to bend over to take off her shiny boots, I can't help but to take in the curve of her ass. She unzips her boots, then pulls them off. She's wearing hedgehog socks. Those little dangling strings move back and forth, accentuating her hips and making her ass look incredible, even if it does look like she's about to do the flamenco or something with those pants. I don't know that Brutus has ever had such fancy pants in his saddle.

Brutus has a speckled faux cowhide, and his horns are a shaped foam so no one actually impales themselves when they get bucked. But it's hard foam and still hurts a bit. The saddle is real, though. There are no stirrups, so you're using your thighs to keep you on. He's got glowing red eyes, a silver ring through his nose, and if he bucks you off, there's smoke that blows from his nose.

"Hey!" Luke says, getting Quinn's attention. attention "Howdy, Quinn. How you been livin'?" *Howdy?* Oh, he's turning on the charm for her. We all chuckle and give him a blatant side-eye.

"Hi, Luke." She looks at him and then at all of us, "Who are your friends?"

"Well you know, Caleb and Jake. I think you met Garrett last year." He points at them respectfully. "And this is Silver Rapids' troublemaker, Maverick." They just laugh it up. No matter what I do, the mistakes of a dumb twenty-year-old are going to follow me everywhere. They laugh, but I don't think they know how much I trained after the accident and then damn near got close to the trials again.

"Nice to meet, y'all. I'm Quinn." She points to where her friend is about to get on the padded mat and walk up to Brutus. "That's my friend-"

"Ladies and Gentlemen, Brutus has a brand new rider coming up to see if she can tame the big bull!" The announcer says over the speaker as her selected entrance song plays. "Gimme More" by Brittany Spears starts playing. "Please put your hands together for Miss Charlotte! Give her some cheers, y'all!" The crowd that's been watching people getting bucked goes crazy when the song comes on.

"That's my babyyyyyy!" Quinn starts hollering at her, jumping, and whistling.

We all give her a good luck cheer. Charlotte had a radiant smile across her face and, in the blink of an eye, morphed into a woman on a mission, her face set in determination. I can see now her eyes are a bright shade of blue. She walks up to the far side of Brutus and hoists herself up with ease. The orange and deep pinks of the setting sun silhouette her frame.

Wow, that move in itself is pretty impressive, but the sight of her settling into the saddle and grabbing the horn–she looks like a natural up there. She gives a nod to the booth attendant and raises her right hand. A buzzer goes off and Brutus starts bucking. Her unbound golden hair is going in every direction, and those little strings of fringe flare out too. There's a heartbeat where she looks like she's about to slide off completely, but to my shock, she's doing a good job of keeping her seat and staying loose. Brutus' bell is ringing with every move that the controller is giving it. It looks like the bull is at full speed and force too. She's counterbalancing with her right hand in the air to counteract the bull's movements, looking like a natural. I thought she would have been bucked in the first few seconds, that this is just something she can say she did to her friends, but I just heard the buzzer signal time.

The bull goes back to the neutral position to allow her to get down. "Ladies and gentlemen, Miss Charlotte just mastered Brutus the Bull!" The announcer shouts into the microphone. "She's the first person all day to hit all eight seconds at full speed."

When he announces this, I turn to my friends who are staring at this girl with their mouths open then back to Charlotte who is jumping down like she's getting out of a big truck and bouncily walks on the mat towards her shoes. Quinn is running towards her shouting, "Hell yes, darlin'!"

I hear Garrett say, "Holy shit, I think I'm in love." Sorry, Garrett, love you like a brother, but that magnificent creature is all mine.

"Again, ladies and gentlemen, give another cheer for Charlotte! Maverick Bennett, if you're here, you're up next!" I hear my name called, and Caleb comes up behind me and pats me on the ass.

"Giddy up, son."

I'm walking over to the entrance when I hear, "I hopped off the plane at LAX..." I stop walking, turn around, and see my entire crew doubled over with laughter. "Sorry, Mav! I had to!" Caleb yells over the music. I am going to kill him. He'll die an unwed, insufferable asshole at my hands, and I'll have to tell Kennedy that he died over a Miley Cyrus song. I love this song, they know it. But that's supposed to stay back a decade or two, everybody loved that song.

I could play this two ways. One, slump my shoulders and sulk at my entrance song when I'm trying to impress the most beautiful woman I've ever seen. Two, I can pretend it doesn't bother me, own it, and get the crowd pumped up. I haven't ever backed down from a challenge in my entire life. So I start to swing my hips to the beat and lift my hands in the air to get the crowd in it with me. The announcer says, "Interesting song choice, but, uh, give ol' Maverick a round of applause. Come on boy, let's see what you got!" They cheer even more as I make my way to the ring entrance. Charlotte is still putting on her boots when I get up to the mat. She turns to me, her gaze starts at my cowboy boots, rises up to my face, and lingers on my eyes. "I would have pegged you for a Zach Bryan man, but Miley's great too." I flash a grin and feel my cheeks warm.

"Uh, yeah, my friends." I motion back to the assholes behind me. "Thought it would be a crowd pleaser." She peeks behind me, covers her smirk with her hand, and giggles.

"The guys with Quinn?"

"Yeah. They're my assholes."

"So many, most guys only have one."

She's got jokes.

"Uh, Maverick, stop flirting with the champion and get on the bull, son," says the announcer. Now I'm getting called out by the damn announcer?

"Go in like a wrecking ball, Maverick," she says and gives me a cheeky little wink. I watch her walk back to the guys and Quinn, her blonde curls bouncing.

I walk up to Brutus, hop up, and put my hand on the horn. I barely have a second to get myself ready before the bull starts going front and down. I probably look like a wet noodle. I'm holding on for dear life. In the words of Miley, we can't stop, we won't stop. Only a few more seconds. That's when I feel like the bull will go right and down, but goes left and up. No, that's me going left and up. I'm going over and land flat on my back, looking up at the clouds left in the sky. Fuck. The crowd is laughing. I feel utterly deflated, like Brutus just took his horns to my ribs and left me on the ground. The white smoke billows out of his nose and the red lights of his eyes shine in the dusk.

I don't hear what the announcer says when I walk back to our group. The guys are laughing, but not Charlotte or Quinn. Charlotte asks, "Yikes. You okay, champ? That looked like it hurt."

"Uh, yeah. I mean, no, it didn't hurt. Maybe just my ego. No one could possibly think to do well after your ride. Have you done that before?"

Confidently, she grins at me and states matter of factly, "No, this was my first time."

I must look at her like I'm a wide-mouthed bass because Garrett comes up and pushes my chin up so fast my teeth clink together. I swat him away.

She laughs and says, "It was just beginner's luck. I've always wanted to try it but none of my friends would ever do it with me." She points a look over to Quinn.

"Your new friend Maverick did it with you," Quinn replies.

"Well, Charlotte 'The Bull Tamer,' can I buy you a drink in exchange for your tips and tricks?"

"Yes!" exclaims Quinn, "But you have to get her cotton candy too. She's the champion. Her time's not free." Charlotte goes into a full blush across her face.

"I feel like you're my madame, selling my time for lemonade and cotton candy," she says to Quinn.

'"Just make sure not to get any funny ideas, mister," Quinn says, waving her finger at me in a stern voice.

"No, ma'am. I'll not do anything untoward."

Quinn eagerly says to the group, "Guys, snacks? Have y'all eaten yet?"

My friends lead us towards the food and, somehow, I feel like I just beat Brutus.

CHAPTER 3

CHARLOTTE

"Baby girl, you looked like a damn rodeo princess riding that bull!" Quinn wraps her arms around my middle and gives me a little shake as we walk down the street towards the food stalls. "I can't believe that was your first time riding a bull like that."

"This actually is my first rodeo," I beam, then add "To be fair, I work with horses every day, Q." I squeak as she squeezes harder.

To the guys ahead of us, she calls, "Y'all, isn't my girl just the prettiest thing to ride Brutus?"

Without meaning to, I sneak a peek up to Maverick from behind my wall of hair. I see his eyes taking me in the way a man does when he's trying to figure you out. His eyes are traveling over my body but when his eyes catch mine watching, he winks.

Garrett says, "She is the prettiest thing this town has ever seen."

Luke slaps Garrett in the stomach, "Aside from yourself, Quinn, ma'am."

"Smooth, real smooth, Garrett," Luke admonishes.

They start ribbing each other and walk ahead of us as they play fight.

"She's not wrong, you know? You looked exceptional on that bull," Maverick has slowed his pace so that he's now walking next to me. "So about those tips and tricks."

I laugh, "I don't know what to say, I don't have any tips for you. I really do think he didn't have it on full force. He let me off easy."

"Bart's guys don't pull punches. If you say go to ten, they go to ten."

"Oh," I'm kind of shocked they would actually do that. The attendant did ask if I had ever ridden a mechanical bull before. I thought he was just being polite and letting me go the full eight seconds. Then the realization sets in that Maverick only went six seconds and I start grinning. Boy is built. Long legs encased in denim that hugs his really, really toned thighs just right. His jeans are faded in a way that comes from regular wear, not the kind that you buy from a store. His hands and muscled arms are veiny. God, I'm such a slut for veiny hands. And he's tall, a few inches well over six foot.

His eyes are a deep blue, like sapphires glistening in the sunshine. His curly hair is a honey brown that's been lightened by the sun at the tips. Unlike Garrett and Luke, he's not in a cowboy hat. But it doesn't take much imagining to see what he would look like with one on... sexy as hell.

"Why are you grinning like a fiend?" He takes a step back and feigns shock, "Should I be frightened?"

"No reason."

"It's okay, you don't have to tell me. I already know," he smirks.

"You do not."

"You're thinking that I purposefully bucked myself off so I could let you seem like a natural. Right?"

I belly laugh at that and say, "That is exactly what I was thinking! You've got me figured out."

We walk in silence for a moment. That's when I notice that Quinn and Luke are now walking next to each other, looking like they're enjoying their conversation because Quinn just said something and Luke is giggling like a schoolgirl.

Quinn has mentioned Luke. He lives in town and goes into the bookstore sometimes and gets books for his mom and Nana. That's cute as hell. She deserves to have someone kind be interested in her. I can recognize the signs of loneliness. I see them often enough when I look in the mirror. Between the loneliness and the paranoia that has me checking the locks on the doors and windows, or out the windows when someone turns the corner a little too slow.

Breaking the silence, Maverick coughs and asks, "Have you been in Silver Rapids long?"

"No. Almost six months or so." Maverick doesn't pry, and I leave it at that. I don't want to share too much with anyone. Even in small towns where I haven't stayed more than a few weeks or a month at a time, I haven't shared too much about myself with anyone. Whenever anyone asked about where I was going or traveling I would answer, 'Just on a summer break. Going on a cross-country trip.' Nothing that would give too much away. It's been ten months since leaving Boston. Since leaving my whole life behind. Ten months of looking over my shoulder.

We get to the food stands and try to decide which line we're going to get in first. When Maverick offered lemonade and Quinn meddled, I could feel my face flush.

I'm curious to learn more about this man. I ask, "You're from here?"

"Yeah, my dad was in the Army as a pilot, thus the name," He gestures to himself. "But I was born in North Carolina and we moved here when I was two. We didn't move around a lot like most Army families though, Dad was already on his way out when my mom got pregnant. Then I was born and he wanted out. His family's from here."

"This place is kind of great. Everyone is so nice and friendly. I've never lived anywhere like it. It's something out of a movie."

"I can see how it seems that way. When everyone knows your grandparents' names and what you did the night before, before your parents even yelled at you the next morning, it can be a bit, uh, stifling."

I never thought of it that way. I had more than two thousand kids in my high school. I don't think there are even that many people in the whole of Silver Rapids.

I get the feeling that he's not a fan of this topic. Just as I get ready to ask about where he currently lives, Quinn comes bounding towards me. "Ma'am, if I asked you to dance with me would you say 'yes'?"

"There's no music playing."

"Well, no, not right now. But Luke was saying that it's Caleb's bachelor party and how we could go to Bart's bar and help them celebrate. He said they wanted to do karaoke, then there's a band playing after. Not just the jukebox."

"Q, it's a bachelor party. We shouldn't impose. Let the guys have their fun."

"Caleb wouldn't care. Kennedy is joining us after her shift at the cafe in an hour or so," Maverick adds.

Turns out I have met Caleb's fiancé before. Kennedy works at the café next to the bookstore. She's been nice to me every time Quinn and I stop in for food during one of Quinn's shifts or on the weekend for brunch.

"Yes! And Caleb was saying she doesn't have anyone to celebrate with so really..."

"Eh, okay, sure. I'll let you push me around the dance floor." She gives me a kiss on the cheek and bounces back to the group ahead of us. If I hadn't been with her the whole time, I could have sworn she was sneaking sips out of a flask or something. Our last drink was a good two hours ago.

"She's got good energy," I say to Maverick.

Watching Luke and her closely, Maverick says, "Luke looks like he's really turning on the charm for your friend. You should watch out for that one, not in a bad way. He tends to be a lady killer and doesn't typically like anything serious. But he'll be a great guy for the right one when he finds her."

Did he just warn me as an out for his friend or was he just being that honest? I take a minute to look into his dark blue eyes. There's no malice in what he's saying. The eyes are what betray people. They can master body language and try to hide their tells, but someone's eyes give away that they're hiding something. I learned that playing poker at my father's country club.

"Thank you for that."

"For what?"

"Being honest."

"How can you tell?"

"You have kind eyes. The eyes tell you everything you need to know."

Maverick doesn't say anything but I can see the gears turning. He probably thinks I'm crazy. "I agree with your theory."

"It's a good one," I say as I meet his blue eyes.

We get to the lemonade stand that also sells candy apples and cotton candy. There are giant bags that are as big as my arm! Two alternating layers of pink and blue sugary clouds. I know cotton candy is just spun sugar, but I love it. He said he was buying my time with sweets. I know it was in jest, but I don't like owing anyone anything. "So about the cotton candy and drinks. You don't owe me anything, it's just all in good fun." His gaze is so piercing.

"I know. But, Charlotte, I'd be honored if you let me buy you copious amounts of dyed sugar disguised as food." He says in a way dripping with sarcasm and a hint of something else.

"Hey!" I say. He smiles and elbows me. I don't know why I share this but I find myself saying, "I wasn't allowed to have this stuff growing up. My parents forbade any sugary substance in the house. Now though, if I want something indulgent, I get it. I appreciate the offer, but I can get my own copious amounts of sugar. "

Quinn and the guys put their orders in and we step up to the window. "The lady will have the big bag of cotton candy." He turns to me, "What to drink?"

Huffing, I put my hands on my hips, "A small lemonade, please."

He grins at me and I return it. He turns back to the window and the young girl taking our order is eyeing Maverick up and down like he's a treat she could devour. Same, girl, same. Maverick's got an ease and way about him, even if he is stubborn. She asks, "And for you?"

"Just water, please. Thank you." He slips her twenty-five dollars, "Keep the change."

"Thank you," I say to him and I mean it. I don't expect anything from anybody. "You didn't have to do that."

"I wanted to," he says, smiling.

We're given our drinks and the giant bag of spun sugary goodness. He is about to hand me my bag when he looks at me and must see the absolute delight written across my face. He cocks his head and smirks, "You look like that one woman who was a game show contestant and ate the whole cotton candy cone in less than two seconds."

I fake indignation at his comment, "You don't know me, I am very competitive, I could take her."

"I just bet you could."

I open the bag and pull out a fluff and bite into it giving a little moan as we walk down through the stalls and I notice more than a few people stop to glare at us. I look down at myself and while the titties are tittying, I'm covered. We pass another table and notice that they're not looking at me but at Maverick. Why though?

I give his sleeve a little tug at the elbow to quietly get his attention and whisper, "Hey. Is it just me or are folks staring at you?"

He takes a deep breath, inclines his head just a bit, and then turns slightly to me. "I have some history here. Seems like people are still pretty upset about it. I thought with enough time away they'd get over it. Looks like I was wrong." He looks so defeated when he says, "It's probably best if you steer clear away from me, especially if you plan on being here for any length of time."

"Did you kill somebody?" I ask him. *Please don't say yes, please don't say yes.*

"No. I just disappointed a whole lot of people."

"Whatever it was, and you don't have to tell me, that sounds like that was on them."

"Easier said than done."

"Honestly, if you didn't hurt or kill someone, could it really be *that* bad? Whatever you did, or didn't do, those disappointed people placed those expectations on you." I say to him, "You're what, like, twenty-five? Twenty-six? If whatever *this* was happened years ago, what kind of people would be mad at you after all this time?"

He doesn't say anything, just looks at me with an intense burning in his blue eyes and says, "This isn't a hornets' nest you want to kick around. I really did disappoint a lot of people." His words have a finality to them, so I don't push the issue any further.

We walk to the group who are currently debating what they want for food. We decide to break off and get in different lines and share amongst ourselves. Caleb and Quinn set off for BBQ. Maverick and Jake head to a chicken sandwich and hamburger grill. I see a stand for pizza. I groan, "Oooh, pizza. Yummy. Anyone else want a slice?" Garrett and Luke shoot their hands up, and we head that way.

Garrett and Luke are talking about riding the bull. Luke says, "Bro, I am telling you, I would have gone the full count this time. We should go back after we eat."

"The only one of us to go the full eight today is Charlotte, here." Garrett gives me a pat on the shoulder.

"Maverick went for eight counts that one time for charity a couple Christmases ago though. Remember?" asks Garrett. "It was a thousand dollars to enter that contest. He got a plastic buckle painted silver, went on the mat to collect the buckle, then fell off the steps from the mat and broke his tooth! And then the drunk fool gave away all his prize money!" They laugh and go on to reminisce about the crazy things they and Maverick did as teenagers.

Ah, so there's definitely more to Maverick than what meets the eye. I tune back in as Garrett is saying, "If you want to get on and ride after eating, that's your choice, but I would think you would want to hang out with Quinn." A lightbulb must have just gone off in his head, because Garrett asks, "Is she why you've been reading so much?" Luke's face turns a glowing red.

I giggle and put my hands up, palms out. "No judgment here, any reason to read is a good one. And... Quinn, could use a reading buddy." I didn't know it was possible for the very tips of someone's ears to glow red too, but Luke's ears look like a beacon.

"Don't tell her, please. I had planned to ask her out the next time I saw her, but the next time was at the grocery market, that's not a vibe. No one wants to get asked out next to the salad dressing. She mentioned that you guys would be going out tonight, and our guys were already here for Caleb's party. I just don't want to ask her for dinner in front of all these assholes. I know you don't know me, but I," he breathes and uncrosses his inky arms. "I really like her. She's got me reading romance books and doesn't even know it. I'm not going to let one of those fictional boyfriend types keep me from shooting my shot."

"Wait, those books are for you?" I ask.

He isn't embarrassed at all. The guy beams, "She's told you about me?"

"Haha, oh, man. Yes, she's told me about this guy who comes into the bookstore to buy books for his mom and nana. I said it was because he wanted an excuse to see her. Turns out I was right." I grin then cross my heart with my hand. "I promise not to tell though."

"Thank you. Thank you!" He looks like he could hug me when he looks over my shoulder and stops abruptly. Pivoting he says, "Next time you need something fixed around your place, let me know. I own a construction company and will absolutely help you out."

We get our pizza order and head back to the tables our friends have commandeered. We share everything on the table and by the time we're slowing down, I've had two pizza slices, some pulled pork, half of Quinn's corn dog, and half a bag of cotton candy.

"I can't possibly eat another thing. I am so full," I exclaim. "Quinn, you're gonna have to roll me home like a tumbleweed."

"Ooh, girl. We're gonna have to take turns rolling each other because I am stuffed as a pig," she drawls.

Luke asks, "The night's just getting started. You guys aren't leaving yet, are you?"

Quinn looks at me and deadpans, "Well, I wanted to stay out tonight. But Miss Charlotte has herself a new job and didn't want to be a bother and ask for the day off tomorrow."

"I feel so bad. I've only worked there for a couple of weeks. Although my boss did say I could have the day off. I just had to text him and let him know."

I haven't even been there long enough to request PTO. I would feel bad about taking an unpaid day too. I never wanna take advantage of anybody. Jasper, my boss, has been so great at helping me get acclimated to being a ranch hand on his property. Growing up around horses didn't necessarily mean that I knew how to muck out their stalls. I just knew how to ride. My version of riding was English style where we focused on jumping, not Western riding. They are very different. If my old riding instructor could actually see me today, throwing around straw bales, he would probably fall over dead.

It's Maverick that says, "If they'll let you take the day, there is usually a big firework display at night over by the drive in."

Considering, I say, "I'll text him. See if I can come in later to start my shift." I say to the table, "Excuse me for one second." I swing my legs around the bench of the picnic table and stand up. Walking over to the garbage and recycling containers, I toss out my plates and napkins, and text Jasper.

Charlotte: *Hi, Boss. I was wondering if I could have a late start to the day tomorrow.*

Boss: *Hello, Lottie. I thought I told you that you were free to take the day tomorrow?*

Charlotte: *You did, but I don't want you to think I'm not trying to pull my weight.*

Boss: *Don't take this the wrong way, but I think it would be good for you to get out and enjoy the day. I'll see you Monday mornin'.*

Well, that's that. "Okay, I'm officially off work tomorrow," I say as I walk back.

Quinn lets out a little whoop, and I take the spot that's open between Garrett and Maverick. They make a little bit more room for me between them. Garrett starts to say something when Maverick says, "Does that mean I can have your first dance?"

I turn to him, he's got a look of earnestness in his eyes. "Yeah, I think I'd like that, Maverick."

Caleb pops up out of his seat, slapping his brother on the shoulder, "Friends, little brother, I think I would like some alcohol. To Bart's?"

Everyone agrees and we head down to Main Street. I don't know how long I'll stay in Silver Rapids. I have no business getting flirty with a man-especially a man I don't know. A man who looks like that. A whiskey sounds great right now.

I've never been inside, but the outside of Bart's looks like an old western saloon. There is a neon sign in the shape of a cowboy and mountains over the sidewalk. It's got double swinging doors and wood paneling everywhere. Pushing through the doors, I'm immediately taken to a what could be the set of an western movie. The place is packed and peanut shells cover the floor of the bar.

"First things first, karaoke!" exclaims an excited Caleb. The guys laugh at him. It's his party. Why shouldn't he be able to sing if he wants to?

"First things first, drinks. Then karaoke, Caleb," Luke quips.

We head to the bar and get the bachelor a shot and a cocktail. The guys shoot those down and head over to the table that's by a band stage. I can hear them argue over which song to pick. When they finally settle on one, they hand the slip in.

Luke announces, "We've got two songs ahead of us. Would you like to dance, Quinn?"

"Yes, sir. I would love to." Quinn turns to me with a huge grin on her stunning face, "You don't mind, do you?"

Shaking my head and returning her grin, I say, "Not at all, give me your bag." I reach out and grab her purse from her. She mouths 'thank you' to me and twirls back to Luke who looks like he has stars in his eyes. Maverick said that Luke was a ladies' man, but he is looking at her with eager yet tender eyes.

A slow country song that's being butchered by this couple on the stage is playing when Luke takes her hand and starts dancing. I'm happy for her. After the song stops, he gives her a spin and they walk back to us, hand in hand.

The next group is called up and sings a Brooks and Dunn song, "Neon Moon." It's such a banger and they're not half bad. Couples are dancing on the floor, and Quinn and I are swaying and singing along. I love karaoke. Back home, before everything, I used to love to go to karaoke nights with the girls and just sing it out.

The group finishes, and everyone is whooping and clapping then our friends are asked to go to the stage. Quinn and I move over to the bar to better see them. Now that the dance floor has more people on it.

They are facing away from us when the song starts, and we burst out laughing. They jump and twist to face forward and land on the beat then walk up to the microphones. They picked a Backstreet Boys song. We're watching the guys sing their hearts out and not one of them can carry a tune in a suitcase, but they all look happy, free from life's worries for a short while. I can tell though, that this is definitely not the first time they have performed this song. And that thought brings up a fit up giggles.

The lights on the stage are changing color to the beat, and they have the biggest smiles on their faces. But even from back here and through the lights, I can feel Maverick's eyes on me. Quinn sees me watching him, watching me.

"I don't know his story, but he seems like a bad mistake you only make once." I'm not sure what she means by that, and I just nod.

I look back to the stage and say, "I think it's an act."

"Oh, no. Charlie, did you just fall in the 'L' word with that beautiful piece of man-meat?"

"Love?!"

"No, baby girl, lust. Lust is fine. But the other 'L' word," she shudders.

"He just doesn't seem like a bad guy."

"Okay, fair," she says. "Like I said, I don't know his story, but he's been giving you eyes all night. And bad guys can still be good men." She raises both her eyebrows and gives them a wiggle. We laugh and try to flag down a bartender to get some cocktails and shots for the guys. I hear their song end and the crowd gives them lots of applause.

I feel a presence behind me. I think it's Maverick, but when I turn around, a man I've never seen before is standing close to Quinn and me. Tall and portly, he's in a plaid shirt and jeans with a trucker hat on. He's too close, the stench of alcohol is so strong coming off his breath that I have to back up a step.

"Hellooo, ladies. How are we doing tonight?" he slurs out to us.

"Um, no thanks," Quinn says as she tries to scoot us around him.

"I'm just trying to say 'hello' to two pretty little ladies. You think you're too good to talk to me?"

We start to walk away but he grabs us both by the upper arms.

"Get your hands off of us, right now," I say. Hoping he doesn't catch the tremble in my voice. His grip on my arm is tight, maybe enough to leave a bruise and I wince when he squeezes.

"How about a ménage dance party?" he says, trying to maneuver us towards the dance floor.

The lights are bright behind the man, so I can't really make out his features. His grip tightens and I am immediately in fight or flight mode. I haven't felt manhandled like this since a few nights before I left home. Quinn and I are squished so tight together and I can feel her shaking next to me. Behind the man I see figures walking towards us.

"Hey!" someone calls from behind him, and the guy turns just a bit, opening himself to me. That's when I jab my knee as hard as I can in his balls and use all of my weight and energy to push him in his chest. He goes down like a pile of bricks, groaning and curled in in the fetal position.

Quinn gives him a good kick to the shins, "Asshole!"

There's commotion when Caleb and Garret go get security. Maverick comes over to us, creating a barrier between the man on the ground and us. "Hey, champ. You guys okay?" I immediately feel better, safer with Maverick between us. My fight or flight has always been more fight, but the adrenaline drop happens quick and I start to think about the what ifs.

"Yes, my girl got him good," Quinn says.

The guys are back with security. Onlookers are trying to see what the hubbub is about, but Maverick and the wall of men are barricading us from everyone. Despite all of my mother's best intentions, I haven't ever needed a man to fight my battles.

Maverick moves to bring his hand on my arm but puts it back down. "Hey," he says to me, a bit softer than before, "are you going to be okay?"

"Yeah, I think. Who was that guy?" That's my bravado talking because I'm taken back to the moment when I was leaving my office, headed for my car, and those two goons stopped me. I would have been whisked away to wherever, but I fought my way free and ran. I've been running ever since.

"I've never seen him before, but I'm sure we can find out. Garrett's dad is the sheriff," Luke says. Obviously I don't know Garrett, but can't picture him growing up with a Sheriff as a dad. He seems like the perpetual prankster. Maybe that's why, he's rebelling, even now. I'm sure it's stifling having a parent in law enforcement.

Quinn seems completely unphased by what just happened. However, I look down and can see the fringes of my top and bottoms jitter, and I realize I'm trembling. Maverick is staring at me, he has to notice. He comes closer to me. "Hey, hey."

I'm quivering, about to have a panic attack. He says in a calm tone, like he's talking to an injured animal, "I'm going to touch you, okay?" I nod and he wraps his arms around me in a hug. Soft, warm, hard, and secure. He says, "Breathe in for four and hold it for four," he pauses, "now breathe out for four and hold it." I do as he says. "That's it. Again."

We stand there just breathing. To anyone else, we might look like lovers embracing, but he's just saved me from a public panic attack, in the middle of a crowded bar, on a Friday night, at the town fair. I don't want to be that girl people whisper about when I go into town for groceries. I feel tears start to fall after a minute or two. I left this life behind, but it didn't leave me.

"There, feel better?"

I wipe my tears with the backs of my hands and say to my new friends and Quinn, "I think I'm calling it a night."

"No, ma'am. That asshat doesn't get to ruin your night out," Quinn replies.

"It's okay. I-," I clear my throat, "Nothing would make me happier than you staying out and shaking that booty being well protected by our new friends and me going home and getting some rest."

Quinn knows about my panic attacks. I had one in front of her a few months ago when I thought I saw one of Father's business associates in the market while we were buying ice cream and popcorn for our movie night.

As though she's remembering that, Quinn says, "Okay, babe. If that's what you want, we can leave right now."

"No!" I breathe, "No, I mean I go home, you stay out with the guys. We can get together tomorrow for brunch."

"I'll walk you home, champ," Maverick says.

"No, look, I don't want to make this about me. Please, stay here, I can get home."

He's got fire in his eyes, as if to say, *Are you kidding? No.*

Quinn looks between the two of us and breaks into a grin just like the Grinch. Then she catches me watching her and schools her features. Like an angel, she sweetly says to Maverick, "That's so gentlemanly of you, Maverick. Thank you for taking care of my girl."

I'm not going to win this one and sigh, "Let me cash out at the bar."

Caleb says quickly, "I've got your drinks. I'm so sorry this happened."

"Sorry to ruin your party," I say to Caleb.

I give them all a quick goodbye, and Maverick and I leave through the saloon-style doors.

We don't talk for a few blocks but it doesn't feel awkward, it's actually kind of peaceful. I look up to the almost full moon watching over us. The lights twinkling, and the scent of wood burning in the bonfire pits set up along the street feels kind of magical.

"I'm sorry we didn't get that dance," I say to Maverick.

"Me too, but I get to walk a beautiful woman back home in the moonlight. No complaints on my end."

He reaches out, and I let him take my hand in his. His palm is calloused and rough in places, but softly he brings it to his mouth and places a gentle kiss atop my knuckles. "I'm sorry you had to deal with all that."

We smile at each other and head back towards my house.

There's still some food and vendor stalls open and a guy playing guitar with a speaker. He must be one of the last performers before the end of the night. He's playing a soft melody that I instantly recognize. It's one of my favorite songs. He must see something on my face, because Maverick pulls me to the small clearing on the street that serves as a makeshift dance floor. He gives me a twirl out then back in, and my hand lands on his shoulder. Then pulls me in with his hand on my waist and we sway gently back and forth without saying a word. The end of the song is coming. He spins me out and back to him close, then dips me backward. He's got moves.

"What street do you live on?"

"Hill, at the corner of Birch."

"I got that dance after all," he says, then brings me upright. The small crowd claps for the singer and we continue to walk. We talk the entire time about everything and nothing at all. Still strangers, yet, I've shared dreams and things I've never been able to share with anyone else in my life. We watch the fireworks from a picnic table in the park. The short walk to my house took hours.

CHAPTER 4

MAVERICK

We come to her street and I don't want the night to end. Charlotte is such an intriguing, enigmatic woman and I want to know more about her, but for as much as we talked, I feel like she's holding a lot close to her chest. I know her favorite color, how she feels about crystals, but I asked what brought her here and she clammed up real quick.

Heading up the stairs to her house, she turns to me as she reaches the top stair. "Thank you for walking me home," Charlotte says. "It's nice to know gentlemen still exist."

"I'm not that good of a guy. I've been trying very hard not to stare at your ass as you were walking up the stairs. I failed."

She laughs, "That doesn't make you a bad man. At least you're honest about it."

"If I'm honest, I would say that I was staring at your ass long before you walked up the stairs. Or that the shade of blue in your eyes is more beautiful than the bluest bluebird sky I've ever seen. Or that I've been wanting to grip your hair and kiss you since the moment I saw you get up on that bull."

At my confession, even in the dark, I can see blush creep up from her slender neck and to her cheeks.

"Um, okay," she breathes. "Thank you for your honesty." Then she yawns, like a full stretch wide open yawn. "Wow, I didn't realize I was so tired. If I made a pot of coffee, would you want a cup? We could just sit out here and swing."

"Swing?"

"Yeah, every good porch needs a swing." She points behind me, and sure enough, there's a white porch swing with lilac pillows. "We could just talk. It's nice out."

"Sure. We can do that." Do I want a cup of coffee? No, but I wouldn't mind getting to know her better.

She unlocks the door and walks into the small house and takes off her shoes. "God, I'm glad to get those off. I haven't worn heels in a minute," she says.

"Should I take mine off?" I'm not presuming anything, and she said we were going back outside.

"Nah, it's okay." But my mother raised me right, I slip them off.

There isn't much in the way of furniture. There's a small gray sofa and a TV console table with some books beneath it. The hardwood floors carry into the open kitchen where Charlotte has started to pull down mugs and gets the coffee pot going. There are wooden bar stools tucked under the kitchen island that I pull out and sit on to watch her work. She's mesmerizing in those pants, even while performing the simple act of making coffee. It looks like she's dancing.

She turns back around and smiles at me. "Are you comfortable there? You can wait on the couch if you want."

"No, I've got the best seat in the house here."

We're at the kitchen island when the coffee maker starts beeping indicating the coffee's done brewing. She's humming something I can't quite name, pulling the coffee mugs from a cupboard. She's not short, but she does have to stretch her long, lean body to reach the back of the cupboard to get the cups down. Then she goes to the fridge and pulls out creamer, chocolate syrup, and whipped cream. My mind goes to a pretty kinky place, but instead of voicing that I ask, "Are you making coffee or hot chocolate?"

"I'm making a mocha. Well, as close to a mocha that I can pull together at this hour at any rate." We laugh. "What do you take in your coffee?"

"Just black."

"Blech. I don't understand it. I can't do that at all. I like my coffee light and sweet."

"Well, ma'am, you'll never have to worry that I'll steal your coffee." *Ma'am? Did that just come out of my mouth?* I inwardly groan at myself.

She smirks at that but doesn't say anything. She makes herself a mocha with the whipped cream about to flow over the sides. She notices the cream falling over the other side and lifts the coffee to her mouth. In the sinful sweep of her tongue, she licks up the length of the cup, lets out a little moan, catches me staring, giggles, then winks at me. She's not even flirting, at least I don't think she is. She's just magnetic, drawing me to her.

"You can't let whipped cream go to waste." My dick just went rock hard in my Wranglers. She hands me my cup and comes around to my side and sits on the stool next to me. The nutty, sweet aroma of the coffee and her sweet caramel and vanilla perfume are a heady mix. I want so badly to put my mouth all over her body, see what she tastes like. I'd bet my life she's as sweet as that cotton candy she loves.

We sit in comfortable silence, sipping on our coffee when we both start talking at the same time.

"Where do you live-"

"What do you do in-"

And then burst out laughing. "You first," I say.

"What do you do in Utah?"

"I'm a ski instructor in Park City." I leave it at that. I don't like to tell people that I was earmarked to join Team USA for the Winter Olympics eight years ago. That on the eve of the biggest night of my life I fell out of a balcony, drunk off my ass. It's kind of nice to not have to explain that to a stranger. It's actually a relief that she knows nothing about me at all. I can try to be the version of me I keep hidden.

"Oh!" She exclaims, "I've never been to Utah, or Park City, obviously, but I have skied quite a bit in Europe, Vail, and in Vermont. Very different types of snow." Has she heard of me? It made the rounds all over ESPN and sports networks, my accidental fall from grace. But she doesn't say anything further. "The photos I've seen on socials from friends have been stunning. You're lucky you get to work in such an awe-inspiring place." *Yeah, lucky my coach hooked me up with the one resort willing to take me on to help kids learn pizza versus french fry.*

Wait, Europe? "Where have you skied in Europe?"

"Chamonix, Zermatt, Saint Moritz."

"Whoa, those are some world-class ski resorts." And some of the most expensive resorts in the world. I am no one to judge, but if I had to, based on the state of furniture and the size of this house, I wouldn't have pegged her for someone with that kind of money.

"Yes, I've been very lucky," she says a bit apprehensively. She takes another sip of her coffee, staring off into a place I can't see. More mystery from this woman. I wait a few heart beats before I realize she's not going to elaborate on that. I don't want to push, but I definitely want to know more about her. You can't say you've been to one of the most well known, most expensive ski resorts and live in the middle-of-nowhere Wyoming without some questions.

"Yeah, I bet you've got some stories to share. Okay, my turn. Where did you move from? What brings you to Silver Rapids?" I ask.

"Nope, a question for a question," she insists.

"Oh! Is that how it goes? Okay." I think about which question to ask her first. "Where did you move from, Charlotte?"

She thinks for a moment, probably debating on how much to share with me. "Massachusetts." A vague answer.

"Where specifically in Massachusetts?"

She sucks her bottom lip into her mouth and bites it. Like she's afraid to answer. "Boston area."

"My turn! Did you really go the whole time on Brutus just to fall off the mat and break a tooth?"

I look away from her and mutter under my breath, "Fucking, Garrett. He told you that story?" I turn to her and she isn't giggling. She is straight up laughing at me. "That's your question? You're wasting a question on that?"

She just breaks out into even more laughter. She's patting the counter-top and kicking her feet. "I'm so glad that you find humor and pleasure in my pain. I didn't know you're a sadist on top of being a bombshell." She goes silent and still. What did I say? "Hey," I put my hand out to touch her, but stop just shy of her shoulder. Maybe she doesn't want to be touched?

But as if sensing my hesitation, she puts her hand on my knee, and smiles. "Yes, that's my actual question." She places her coffee mug back down and stands up. "But let me tell you why. The guys said it was for charity. That the proceeds went to a family in need in the next town whose house burned down during Christmas.”

“Maybe, I just wanted to prove I was the best,” I boast.

“You wanted to pay a thousand dollars to win a little, plastic, gold buckle to prove you could go the longest without getting bucked off? I don't believe that.” She inches closer to me and leans in to whisper in my ear, her breath tickling the hairs along my nape. She continues, “I think you wanted to help that family and not let anyone see beyond the bad boy vibe you're trying to put out.” Fuck. “But your secret is safe with me.”

Then she wraps her hands around my shoulders and gives me a kiss on the cheek. And walks around to the sink. Fuuuck. I'm so gone for this girl, this woman. How was she able to read me so clearly? No one ever would suspect me of trying to be the good guy.

I felt so bad watching the news at Dad's and seeing that the Christmas tree caught fire and then spread to their home. The two kids were maybe five or six, and the parents looked devastated. That shit tugged on my heartstrings. When the guys wanted to go out and let off some steam, I suggested Bart's bar and donated for an entry. The guys thought I was being reckless with money. They never read me like she did just now. Simple as a book. In that single observation, she may know me better than anyone in my life does.

She rinses out the cup and places it in the dishwater. I stand up and go over to the sink, towering over her short frame and dumping out the coffee at the same time.

“Don't go sharing that secret. We don't need the town thinking I'm anything other than what they already think of me.” I say, putting the cup in the dishwasher and closing it.

She is just looking at me with curious eyes and asks, “Why?”

“It's just easier that way. I'm the asshole.”

"You're not, it's just easier for you to play the role you were given. I think you're kind of great."

We stare at each other for a moment. I'm taking in her soft, full lips, sharp jaw, and high cheekbones. I move my hand to grip her hip. She shifts her weight to her other foot away from my hand.

"I don't hook up on the first night. That's not what I'm looking for. I don't know what this is because you're going home and I don't know if I'm staying, but I'm not a hit it and quit it type," she says.

"Another honest moment," I take a breath, "this feels like something real. You might be the first real thing I've ever had my hands on." I mean it too. It's not just a line to get her on her back.

She takes it in. Leans her forehead on my chest and just stands there a minute with her hands on my waist. I'm still gripping the sink ledge when she looks up to me with those sky blue eyes.

"It feels like something," I say to her. Charlotte looks optimistic. Her face has a brightness to it. "I think you're one of the most beautiful souls on the planet. The outside, the packaging, is a perk, but who you are inside, you're extraordinary."

She continues, "If we do this, just promise me one thing: not to make it a one and done thing." I know what she's asking, and maybe for the first time, there's a reason for me to come back home more often.

I look down into her eyes, taking in their deep blue depths. I nod. "I understand what you're saying. I feel like I was meant to come back and find you." I lift her by her waist to the counter. "But I can't guarantee that long term I'll be anything but bad for you. I'm still working on pieces of me."

"I've got demons too. Things that I am too afraid to see in the mirror. I'm not asking for forever from a man I just met, but I believe things and people come into your life for a reason. I don't know what that reason is yet, but I'd like to find out and see where this takes us."

"Yeah, I'm on board for that," I agree.

I slide my hands slowly up from her slender waist up to her ribs and back down as I lean in and take her mouth with mine in a soft, exploring kiss. She opens for me and deepens the kiss. Her legs that were bracketing my body are now wrapped around me, pulling me closer to her. I bring my hands to her hips and ass and squeeze. She makes a little squeak. Oh. She likes that. I do it again and grip her hips harder, and she moans louder. I'm going to love peeling back every single layer of this woman and finding out what she likes, what she wants. I've enjoyed the darker, more rough side of sex, and fuck if I wouldn't love to tie her up, but I want to live in this moment with her.

"You feel so good." I say as I break our kiss. Her skin is so smooth, but I start to feel goosebumps as I trail my fingers up her spine and grip her neck to expose it to me.

"God, it's been forever since anyone has touched me," she replies.

I move my mouth to her ear and suck the tip into my mouth and earn a little breathy moan.

"Maverick, that feels good."

She's greedy and I haven't even touched her properly. I move my kisses down the column of her throat, and when I get to where her neck and shoulders meet, I give her a little bite. Not enough to leave a mark but enough to get her attention.

She cries out, "Oh!"

I think, not yet, but you'll be giving me a proper "Oh," soon. Her hands are tangled in my hair, and she's giving just the slightest little tug. There she is.

I straighten as I move my hands behind her back and start to undo her top. Looking at her mouth that's just barely parted, she's panting. The top is held together by a bow style that comes undone with just a little tug. This thing stayed on while she rode Brutus? The straps loosen and without breaking eye contact, I slide the straps down her arms and let the top fall to her lap and put it on the counter. I'm just a man, I look down to the most exquisite breasts I've ever seen. Her perky nipples are dusky pink, and her luscious breasts are perfect teardrops.

When I drag my gaze to her eyes, she's watching me. I move my hands to cup her neck and bring her to kiss me. With the backs of my hands, I graze my knuckles down her front and over her tight nipples then cup her full breasts. The full weight in my palms push out with every big breath she takes. I run my thumb around the pebbled peak and take the other in my mouth and suck, and graze with just a little teeth. I think she was into it when I bit down on her neck. This is just to test it out. Going into this situation without any type of alcohol is certainly a different type of experience. To be fully present with a lover, particularly someone like Charlotte, is new for me. I hope to God this is just the first of many times I get to have her like this.

She's trailing her fingers through my hair. I give her nipple a little bite, then flick with my tongue to soften the sting. She moans louder. When I move my mouth to her other breast and flick my tongue across it, I pinch her other nipple ever so lightly and roll it between my thumb and forefinger.

"Yes, just like that. I like that," she says breathily, and my cock, which was already hard, goes into steel mode.

I pull back a bit and straighten. Looking at her, I ask, "Do you like a bit of pleasure and pain, sweetheart?"

Her face instantly heats and goes red, then looks down and away from me. Almost as if she's ashamed to admit what she likes in bed. "None of that now. This works if you're honest with me," I say.

I grab her chin with my thumb and forefinger and make her look at me. "I will never, ever make you feel ashamed for telling me what makes you feel good. What makes you feel empowered. Or for telling me what your nastiest fantasies are. Now, tell me, what do you like?"

A heartbeat, then two. I think she's not going to respond when she says, "I do like it a bit rough. But whenever I tried to introduce new things-oils, toys, or new things in the bedroom to spice it up a bit, the guys in my past were never into it."

I drop my hand from her face to the tops of her thighs. I'm a bit shocked that any man would deny her anything, especially pleasure.

"Boys are afraid of toys and 'new things' that make them feel inferior. Men understand that toys, they're our best wingmen. I'm not intimidated by silicone as long as I'm the one that gets to watch you play or lend a helping hand."

"Unfortunately, that's never been my experience," she confesses, looking more than a little dejected.

"We can change that. We can do whatever you like, however you'd like."

She pauses for a few breaths. "I have a few things I'd like to try upstairs," she says much more confidently.

I can't even begin to imagine what kind of things she'd like to try, but I'll give her whatever she wants tonight. I don't know where it's coming from, but this primal beast that's been dormant in me for so long starts to come to the surface and wants to claim her.

"Help me out of these?"

I try to feel around for the zipper of her pants. I give a little tug and nope, those aren't pull-ons. She giggles. "It's invisible." She hops down and brings my hand to her hip. "You see, it's just here."

"I never would have found that. I would have sooner cut your pants off."

"These are kind of irreplaceable. So, I would appreciate it if you just slid the zipper down carefully and save the scissors for another day." She gives a coy grin and helps me take her pants down. I feel like she's getting bolder from where we were just a few minutes ago.

She wiggles her hips a bit, and the fringes swish as she pushes them off. I'm kind of mesmerized by the back and forth movement, like a snake caught in trance, but as soon as the pants make it past her hips, my eyes latch on to the slightest sliver of white lace peeking from under the waistband. I snap my hands to hers. "Let me."

I lower myself slowly, settling down onto my heels and look up at Charlotte. I gently reach my hands out and pull her pants unhurriedly down her legs, my eyes watching a trail of goosebumps raise from her skin where my fingers graze. She watches me and looks like she knows she has the power here. I'm practically on my knees for her. I help her step out of her pants and lift her foot to rest on my knee. I kiss the inside of her knee, dragging my nose and lips along her skin, up her inner thigh. I inhale her scent and place another kiss on her lace-covered pussy.

"Maverick," she says, as a warning or a plea, I'm not sure. I place her foot down and stand up. I'll let her decide how far she wants to take this tonight. "You seem awfully overdressed," she says and she reaches for the top button of my shirt. With steady hands, she unbuttons the first few.

After the third button, I put my hand on hers and say, "This can be just about you. We don't have to do anything you don't want to do."

She continues to unbutton my chambray shirt. When she reaches the bottom button, it's my turn to watch her appreciate my hours in the gym and on the slopes. I'm not a big and bulky gym bro, but I am toned and sculpted after decades of training. Her appreciative gaze lingers on my lower abdomen, and then she sweeps her gaze up my chest as she pushes the shirt off my shoulders. I let it fall to the floor.

Finally, looking up to my eyes, she says, "I appreciate that, but I like giving too." Then she slides her hand to my dick strained in the denim. When she feels just how big I am, she gives an appreciative smile.

Damn, if that's not kryptonite. I'm a bigger guy that's blessed in that department, but I never want to push a woman into something she's not comfortable with, unless that's what she asks for. She's naked except for her white, lace, cheeky panties. I look at her body, admiring the magnificent curves and planes. And, if I'm honest, I feel like I can see past her skin, down into her soul. It's kind of terrifying, in a wondrous way.

She's light on her feet as I pick her up and carry her to the island and lay her out on it. Her blonde waves fan out around her head. She sticks her tongue out and runs it along her bottom lip as I place her feet on the wooden countertop. Her eyes go big as I spread her legs and glide my hands from her ankles to under her calves and then to the top of her thighs, stopping when I reach the lace. The lights are on above us, highlighting the curves of her body and her high cheekbones. Not breaking her gaze, I slowly slide the scrap of lace to the side and see just how wet Charlotte is for me.

I skim the pad of my thumb along her center and dip it in between her folds to feel the wetness gathered there.

"Is this for me, Charlotte?" I bring my thumb to my mouth and lick it off. "Mmm, you taste divine, like a delicacy."

I love that her eyes are on me as I bring my mouth to her center and use the broad part of my tongue lick from her opening to her clit. It's then that she closes her eyes and arches her neck and back and brings her hands to her breasts and plays with her nipples. God, watching her do that while I'm between her legs is a damn sight and makes my cock strain against my jeans.

"Charlotte," I say as I take her right hand in mine. "Show me how you touch yourself. Show me how you tease that pretty pussy." I feel the resistance and she instantly tries to pull her hand back to her chest. "I've got you. Show me how you like it."

She looks at me with hesitation but gives the slightest nod. The vulnerability in her eyes makes me so angry, I want the names of the assholes who made her feel this way. I gently guide her hand from between the valley of her breasts to her folds. Once there, she pauses, takes a breath and bares herself to me. She circles her clit and is cupping her mound under the thin lace of her panties. I can't help but stare at her. She inserts a finger into her sex and then another, slowly at first then a bit faster, hurried. I swear she's doing this under her panties to get a rise out of me.

Still between her legs, I'm watching her bring herself pleasure. I gruffly say, "Good. That's a good fucking girl." Her fingers are still deftly dipping in and out of her center and her face is flushed, whether by excitement or nervousness I'm not sure, but she's watching her hand and that's hot as fuck. God, I can't take this torture anymore.

I didn't want this to be about me, but I bring her closer towards me and the edge of the counter, then push her legs wider and over my shoulder. I take her fingers still slick with her essence and put them in my mouth to suck them clean. Giving her back her hand, I open her pussy with one hand, the other still holds her panties to the side, and flick my tongue over her bundle of nerves softly, playing. She's moaning my name, "Mav! Oh, fuck." I alternate between the long strokes and flicks. I all but rip these panties off her body and toss them to the floor.

She is soaking, and when I insert my forefinger and make a come here motion inside her while circling her clit with my thumb, I can feel her start writhing on my hand. I insert a second finger and suck on her clit while moving them in and out using that same come here motion. Working faster and faster. The combination of my fingers and mouth take her higher and higher.

"Yes. Oh God, yes!" I can feel her walls start to quake and squeeze. After a few more licks, I feel a sudden rush of liquid on my face. It is unexpected and so goddamn hot, I might just come in my jeans.

"Oh my God. Oh my God. I'm so sorry. Oh my God." Charlotte groans into her hands that are now covering her face, embarrassed.

"Why are you embarrassed? That was so fucking hot!" It wasn't a lot like I've seen in some of those spice videos where she soaks the bed.

"I've, uh, never done that before."

"Like, never?"

"No." She shakes her head. "There's only been a few times I've ever had anyone eat-" she blushes and groans, "Uh, not all of my partners liked to, uh, lick, down there."

I take a look down again at her perfect sex before me, then back to her face. I pull her hands off her face. "That's a damn shame. You're a treasure, Charlotte, and fuck every man who has ever made you feel less than what you deserve."

I lick my lips and still feel some of her juices on my face. "The fact I could bring you to such an intense orgasm that you squirt on my face is the hottest thing to ever happen to me. I could be near death and still remember this moment."

I can tell I shocked her with that admission. She moves to sit up and I pull her to an up position and she scoots closer towards me and surprises me. She cups the back of my neck, bringing her mouth to mine in a searing kiss. With our tongues stroking back and forth, I know she can taste herself on my tongue, on my lips. The thought of her enjoying the taste shoots straight to my toes.

She pulls back for a moment. "Thank you for not making me feel ashamed."

I hold her gaze for seconds or for a lifetime. Somewhere inside the darkest part of my heart, I think I just felt an ember spark to life. This woman has no idea just how badly I want to reprogram all the things she's learned about sex or her body by men who didn't have a clue. Show her how fucking phenomenal sex can be with the right partner. That I might be her right partner. How it can make you bolder and empower you to feel like you can take on the world. I want to bring this woman to the edge over and over again. I want to bury my cock so deep in her and fuck those negative thoughts right out of her brain.

"That's nothing to be ashamed of, sweetheart." Then I slide my hands under her ass and toss her over my shoulder as I head up the stairs to what has to be her bedroom. I smack her ass hard for good measure and get a little yip out of her. Her curled, mussed hair bounces on the backs of my legs. What I've got planned for her upstairs though, I want to test just how far my little vixen is wanting to take this tonight.

EPILOGUE

The sunrise is shining through the white lace curtains and on to Charlotte's beautiful face, casting shadows under her eyes from her long lashes as she blinkingly opens her eyes to me. Those eyes that bored into mine as she took my hand and wrapped it around the front of her neck as I pistoned into her from below. We only finally went to sleep about an hour or so ago, and I know she's tired. I know she didn't fake all those orgasms. I wish I could stay with her and continue our conversation from last night.

Admittedly, we talked all night in between rounds of pleasure when she laid on my chest, and I twirled strands of her golden hair around my finger. Or when we laid side by side looking at the constellation she painted on her ceiling talking about our favorite childhood memories. She loved riding horses, and I loved getting up on skis anytime I could.

I have to leave her though. Dad needs my help today, and I'm really not looking forward to hearing about how I am never around to help him anymore. I give her a soft kiss to her forehead then to her lips and put on my clothes. She starts to get up, "No, stay, sweetheart. Get some rest. I'll see you tonight."

She mumbles with a smile on her face, "I can't wait. You'll lock up? I think I need a few more hours before I can move." I give her a lingering kiss before I head downstairs.

Last night was incredible. I don't know what type of alternate universe I woke up in, but for the first time I feel something other than self-loathing. Before leaving Charlotte's house, I make her a fresh pot of coffee, get a mug down from the cupboard, and look around for scissors. I look all over this kitchen and not a single drawer has a pair of scissors. I grab a chef knife from the small knife block, quietly open the front door, and cut off a few of the wildflowers growing near the porch, try not to slam screen door, and put them in a water glass. I think to write her a note. I find a notepad and a pen in one of the drawers and scribble, "Enjoy the sunshine today!" Then rip it off the pad, crumple it, and slip it in the front pocket of my jeans. That sounded so stupid. Be smooth, man, don't blow this. Instead, I write, "Last night was incredible! -X- Maverick." Locking the door, I close it gently to not wake her up.

I make my way down her block towards where I left the Jeep behind Mrs. Clark's bakery. I have a huge grin on my face when I pull out my phone and text her.

Maverick: *Have the best day off and rest up, gorgeous. I can't wait to see you for dinner tonight.*

I know she's probably already fallen back asleep, and I don't expect a text back right away, I just wanted her to know I was excited to see her again tonight. When I see the little notification that says "Delivered" I slip the phone back in my pocket and try get my head right to spend a full day of dealing with my dad.

What happens after Maverick walks away? Find out in Charlotte and Maverick's book, Anastasia Wilder's full-length debut novel, releasing in Spring 2025.

ACKNOWLEDGEMENTS

First, and most importantly, I would like to thank my exceptional husband for being the very first person on Team Wilder. No one tells you what your partner experiences when you decide to start writing, but from day one your unwavering support, constant encouragement, long hours of analysis and character development, and the absolute patience you had during my late-night writing sessions, has been nothing short of remarkable. The comedic relief alone has been incredible. You've been there to remind me that all my dreams are possible and this book is in the world because you encouraged me to chase what I want. I love you more than all the words, bun.

A very special thank you to my FBS and KTW girlies. I am so grateful to have found an amazing, talented, and supportive community of writers. Thank you for the advice, sprint sessions, and celebrations of small and big wins. To my PA, Mads, thank you for organizing my chaos.

To my Bad Girls, you have been my biggest champions, from the bottom of my heart, thank you!! To Chelsea, there's a lot of who we are in these stories, the adventures we've collected over the years. I love you. To the Good Girls, thank you. You all are the jelly to my peanut butter, the hot to my honey and I am blessed to have your friendship and unwavering support.

To the readers- thank you for taking a chance on a wee baby author who had a dream, chucked it out the window, and wrote this novella instead. To me, time is the most precious gift and I am so honored that you spent some of yours with me in this world I've created. I hope you enjoyed a sneak peek into Silver Springs.

The writing journey is wild. I never set out to write a dark, small town, cowboy romance, I was 40K deep into a dark, romantic suspense when I had to write a short, extended introduction to a story that was on the horizon. This story was inspired by a video I saw early this year about skijoring, when I saw this badass woman riding a horse down the icy, snow-covered street in Colorado. I had the full-length novel plotted within a few hours, and Midnight Heatwave was born from building the backstory. The Cozy Chronicles Anthology piece took me out of NYC and right into Wyoming, I was just along for the ride. It was a pivot that I never saw coming, but I am loving where I am with these stories.

And finally, to the residents of Silver Springs- you assholes took over my life and kept me in a chokehold. You weren't supposed to be published first but somehow it worked out exactly as it was supposed to. I'm sure my og characters, Beatrix and Gabriel, would have some shit to say about it, but writing you helped me become a better writer so I could give them more time they deserve to marinate in my head.

ABOUT THE AUTHOR

Anastasia Wilder is a dark romance author whose passion for storytelling and reading began at a young age. Her love for dark romance, suspense, and romantasy fuels her writing, bringing a unique blend of intensity and emotion to her stories. Anastasia's journey as a writer started when she was inspired by a dress, imagining a story that she soon wove into a captivating plot about a conservator at the Met Museum, but after her own plot twist she didn't see coming, she started working on a novella that quickly captivated all of her attention!

Anastasia lives in Midwest with her husband and two fur babies. When not simping over morally grey men, wing leaders, guys with wings, or the villain, she enjoys skiing, traveling to new places, and swinging in her hammock with a cocktail in hand.

For other upcoming projects, art reveals, and shenanigans, sign up for Ana's newsletter on her website: www.authoranastasiawilder.com You can also follow Anastasia Wilder on Facebook, Instagram, and TikTok: @authoranastasiawilder. Email your thing? You can reach her at anastasia@authoranastasiawilder.com